A LIGHT IN THE DARK

A CALLAHAN CHRISTMAS

Special Thanks

This novella is a little different, told in a new tone and from a fresh point of view, yet still rooted in the world readers love. Don't worry: the usual Callahan family chaos, danger, and gritty survival will return in full force with the next novel arriving in January.

This project holds a special place in my heart because of the incredible young artists who helped bring it to life. Every piece of artwork attributed to Fiona in this story was created by three talented student artists from the Sayre Area School District. Their creativity, professionalism, and enthusiasm made this collaboration an absolute joy.

To the students: thank you for lending your gifts to this world and for approaching the work with such heart.

To their teacher, Ashley Koopman, who supported the project: your guidance and encouragement shine through every page.

I'm honored to have partnered with you. Thank you for making this novella something truly unique.

TABLE OF CONTENTS

CHAPTER 1: LILY

The wagon wheels crunched through fresh snow, a rhythm that matched the heartbeat of anticipation pulsing through the cousins. Lily tugged the quilt higher, snowflakes falling on her eyelashes as she peered ahead. She carefully tucked her notebook into her pocket so the pages would stay dry. The Lodge appeared like something from a storybook; smoke curling from the stone chimney, windows glowing amber with candlelight and oil lamps.

"Look, look!" Fiona nudged her sister, Rowan, pointing with mittened hands. "Gran's got her red shawl on. The one with the soft tassels!"

Pop had ridden ahead to let everyone at the Lodge know they were on their way home. He was back well before the wagon rolled into the driveway.

Pop stood tall beside Gran on the porch, his broad silhouette backlit by the warm glow spilling from the open door. His hands rested on Gran's shoulders, and even from a distance, Lily could see how Gran leaned into him, her cane planted firmly in the weathered boards beside her.

"I think Odin sees us," Lily whispered to Fiona, spotting the massive Bernese Mountain Dog's wagging tail behind Gran's skirts.

The wagon slowed, her father's booming rendition of "Deck the Halls" faded as Uncle Boone pulled the horses to a stop. Ian clapped his mittened hands one final time before he scrambled to stand up.

"Careful, buddy," Dad called, steadying his son.

"GRAN! POP! We got the BIGGEST tree!" Ian's voice rang across the snowy yard.

Pop's laugh rumbled down from the porch. "Well, now, let's show Gran the mighty forest giant you've conquered!"

Franklin reached up to help Fiona, Rowan, and Lily down from the wagon.

"Careful of the ice sweetheart." he said to Lily as she headed toward the porch.

"I will, Daddy," Lily said as she kissed his cheek.

The children tumbled from the wagon like puppies, boots crunching in snow, voices rising in a chorus of excited chatter. Merryn, still clutching her half-eaten cookie, rushed ahead with surprising speed for such small legs.

Gran opened her arms as the children reached the steps. "My treasures," she murmured, bending carefully to embrace them. "Did you leave any pine trees standing in our woods?"

Lily breathed in the familiar scent of vanilla and herbs that always clung to Gran's clothes. "We found one that's perfect, Gran. I bet it touches the ceiling in the great room!"

"It would have looked amazing with colored lights," Fiona added, then brightened. "But Pop promised we'd have candles this year!"

"Carefully," Gran reminded them with a wink. "Very carefully. Probably not actually in the tree."

Pop surveyed the wagon piled high with greenery and pine. "Looks like Christmas to me," he said softly, his weathered face creasing into a smile. "And I don't need electric lights to see that."

Zeke inspected the massive pine with an appraising eye. Buck joined him, rubbing his mountain man beard and raising an eyebrow.

"Well, I'll be," Zeke muttered, circling the tree. "This one's got more girth than old Widow Parker's prize-winning pumpkin last harvest." He tapped the trunk with gnarled knuckles. "Solid as a miser's heart, too."

Buck nodded his agreement, producing a low whistle. "Gonna take four men to wrestle this beast inside."

Pop said as he clapped his son on the back, "This one really is a fine specimen, Franklin, even if it wasn't the tallest. Reminds me of the year we cut down that blue spruce that took out half the dining room when it fell over."

"I remember that!" Judith laughed. "Ma almost made you sleep in the barn for a week."

"Pssh, I would have let him back in after three days," Gran corrected with a wink. "I'm not completely heartless."

Ian tugged at Pop's sleeve. "Did the tree really break the house?"

"Only the furniture," Pop ruffled the boy's hair. "Nothing your Uncle Owen, your Dad, and I couldn't fix."

The family gathered around the wagon, reaching for decorations and greenery as the scent of pine filled the air and the promise of warm drinks and laughter waited inside.

Franklin and Owen hopped onto the wagon bed, working to untie the ropes that secured the magnificent pine.

"Careful now," Mary cautioned as Ruth and Fiona darted between the adults, snatching up fallen pine boughs to clutch to their chests.

Lily watched her father's face in the fading afternoon light, the way his eyes crinkled at the corners when he smiled down at Ian. There was something different about him this Christmas – about all the adults, really. A quiet determination behind their laughter.

"Gran says we're making popcorn strings tonight," Rowan announced, helping to gather smaller branches. "And she's teaching us to dip pinecones in wax for the mantle."

Beth emerged from the Lodge carrying a tray of steaming mugs. "Hot apple cider for the lumberjacks," she called, her breath visible in the cold air.

"Just in time," Boone replied, kissing her cheek as he took two mugs to share with Zeke and Buck.

The sun dipped lower behind the mountains, turning the snow-covered ground golden-pink. Odin bounded through the drifts, barking excitedly as Pop and Franklin finally freed the tree from its bindings.

"Everyone ready?" Pop called out.

The family formed a line, hands reaching for branches and trunk, faces bright with expectation. In that moment, with the Lodge glowing behind them and the pine needles sharp and fragrant against their mittened hands, it felt like Christmas had already arrived.

The children stampeded into the lodge, boots thundering against the wooden floor as snow melted into puddles. Coats, hats, and mittens flew in every direction as they shed their winter layers like butterflies emerging from cocoons.

"Hot chocolate by the fire!" Aunt Clare called, attempting to corral the excited children toward the kitchen. "And mind the—", her warning came too late as Ian skidded across the entryway in sock feet, landing with a soft thud against a pile of winter gear.

On the wide staircase overlooking the great room, Lily, Fiona, and Ruth had claimed the perfect vantage point. Lily's pencil flew across the pages of her notebook, capturing the perfect words to describe the beautiful chaos unfolding before them.

"Dad's face is turning bright red," Ruth observed, bouncing excitedly between her cousin and sister. "Look how they're trying to turn the tree sideways! It's still too big!"

"Stop moving so much," Fiona muttered, tongue peeking out in concentration as her chalk scraped across paper. Her fingers were already stained blue and green from capturing the massive pine tree being manhandled through the doorway.

"They need to angle it more," Lily murmured without looking up from her notebook. "Uncle Boone's going to hit the—"

A sharp crack echoed through the lodge as a branch caught the antler chandelier, setting it swinging.

"Careful!" Gran called from her armchair near the fire. "Augustus Callahan, if you break my chandelier after all these years—"

"Just a gentle nudge, Jo," Pop grunted, hands gripping pine bark. "Franklin, lift your end higher!"

"Any higher and I'll need a ladder," Franklin shot back, face flushed with exertion.

Ruth giggled, bouncing harder. "Uncle Tobias looks like he's going to drop it!"

"He's just being dramatic," Fiona said, smudging green chalk across her drawing with her thumb. "The dads and uncles all have a flair for the dramatic in this family."

Lily scribbled faster and giggled. "I'm writing that down."

The massive tree finally cleared the doorway with a shower of needles and snow. Mary quickly slid the tree stand into position while Beth directed traffic with the authority of a drill sergeant.

"Two inches left! No—your other left, Boone!"

Lily captured it all, the laughter, the frustrated grunts, the children darting between adult legs. This was what she loved most about her family: the beautiful, chaotic symphony they created together.

"Someday," she whispered to her notebook, "I'll write a whole book just about Christmases at the Lodge."

* * *

The kitchen transformed into a battlefield of flour, sugar, and organized chaos. Every surface gleamed with preparation – jars lined up for jam, cookie sheets stacked high, and measuring cups positioned like soldiers waiting for commands. The aunts moved with practiced precision, directing their young charges with the efficiency of generals.

"Attention, cookie brigade!" Gran called from her chair at the head of the massive wooden island. She tapped her cane against the floor, and children's heads swiveled toward her like sunflowers tracking the sun. "Operation Sugar and Spice is officially underway."

"Team Gingerbread, follow Aunt Beth! Team Sugar Cookie, with Aunt Clare! Jam-makers, come with me," Mary announced, clapping flour-dusted hands.

Lily stood at attention beside Fiona, watching as Jake and Sadie joined their jam-making squad. Gran wandered from station to station, Odin at her heels, giving encouragement, help, and praise in abundance.

"Christmas jam is serious business," Gran informed them, her eyes twinkling. "Been making it the same way since before your parents were born. Well, not exactly the same. Pssh, to be honest, I change it all the time." She laughed as she walked over to the jam station. She said in a hushed, conspiratorial tone, "You can add or subtract depending on what you like and don't like. Nobody will know…there are no kitchen police!"

"The secret," Gran told Lily and Fiona, "is equal parts patience and rebellion. This recipe has been in our family for five generations, but I've changed it practically every year depending on what I have in the pantry. Pretty soon, we will have to make a change for when our freeze-dried citrus runs out."

Rowan and Leah, the teenage cousins, moved through the kitchen like mischievous spirits. Rowan approached Lily with a handful of flour.

"War paint," she declared solemnly, tracing two lines across Lily's cheeks. "For strength in battle."

Leah did the same to Fiona, who giggled and squirmed as flour dusted her nose. Soon, every child sported flour streaks, a badge of belonging to the Christmas baking brigade.

Lily carefully extracted her notebook from her pocket, flipping to a clean page. Mary noticed and smiled.

"Want to be our official recipe keeper?" she asked, passing Lily a weathered recipe card. "This one's seen better days."

The card, stained with decades of spills and spots with Gran's handwriting, held the sacred Christmas jam recipe. Lily's heart swelled with importance as she began copying it carefully, recording each ingredient and instruction in her neatest handwriting.

"Cranberries, oranges," she whispered as she wrote. "Cardamon—Gran's secret touch."

Gran's Ever-changing Christmas Jam

as recorded by Lily Callahan

12 Oz Cranberries (fresh or frozen, thawed if frozen)
1 Orange, peeled and sectioned
2 teaspoons Orange Zest, from the peel
16 Oz Strawberries (fresh or frozen, thawed if frozen) or your choice of berries
¼ teaspoon Ground Cloves
¼ teaspoon Ground Cinnamon
1/8 teaspoon Allspice
1/4 teaspoon Cardamom
4 Cups pure cane sugar (or 3 cups honey: see notes)
1 - 1.75 Oz Package Powder Fruit Pectin
½ Cup Water
½ teaspoon butter (optional, helps reduce foaming)

Prep jars and canner. Wash jars, lids, and rings in hot, soapy water. Rinse well. Keep jars hot (around 180°F) in your canner until ready to fill. Set lids and rings aside in a bowl of hot water.

Add cranberries and orange sections to a blender or food processor and pulse until coarsely chopped. Add strawberries, zest, and spices; pulse again until finely chopped but not pureed.

Pour the fruit mixture into a large, heavy pot. Stir in water, pectin, and butter. Bring to a full rolling boil over high heat, stirring constantly.

. Stir in all the sugar (or honey). Return to a hard boil and boil exactly 1 minute, stirring continuously.

Remove from heat and skim any foam if needed. Ladle hot jam into hot jars, leaving ¼-inch headspace. Wipe rims clean with a vinegar-dampened cloth, center lids, and tighten bands fingertip-tight.

Lower jars into a boiling water-bath canner, making sure they're covered by at least 2 inches of water. Process for 10 minutes (check your altitude!). Turn off the heat, remove the lid, and let jars rest in the water for 5 minutes. Move jars to a towel-lined counter and let cool undisturbed for 24 hours.

Check seals and store. After 24 hours, test the lids. Store sealed jars in a cool, dark place for a year or more. Refrigerate any unsealed jars and use within 3-4 weeks.

After the 1st batch, taste and adjust spices as needed.

Lily was ready to plunge her hands into the sticky, sweet work of making memories.

Around her, the kitchen hummed with activity. Fiona stood on a stool, crushing cranberries with a wooden pestle, her tongue poking out in concentration just like when she was drawing. Jake measured sugar while Sadie sorted and measured spices, the homey scent of cinnamon in the warm air.

From the other side of the kitchen came the spicy aroma of gingerbread as Team Gingerbread mixed molasses and cinnamon. Team Sugar Cookie rolled dough with tiny hands, flour clouds rising with each enthusiastic press.

Lily finished copying the recipe and tucked her notebook safely away. She looked up to find Gran watching her, a soft smile on her face.

"Now you're part of the tradition too," Gran said quietly. "Keepers of stories and keepers of recipes – they're not so different, are they?"

The kitchen windows steamed over, creating a cocoon of warmth against the snowy world outside. Beyond the glass, the men could be seen stringing long boughs of greenery along the porch railings, their breath visible in the cold air.

* * *

11

The long dining table had been cleared of dinner dishes and transformed into a crafting station. Mom and Aunt Ellie moved between the children, offering guidance and encouragement as small hands worked with natural treasures gathered from the forest.

Baskets overflowed with treasures gathered from the autumn woods: milkweed pods still holding their silky filaments, pinecones of every size, dried herbs bundled with twine, and slices of dried orange that glowed like stained glass when held up to the lamplight.

"Look what I found in my craft stash," Aunt Mary announced, unveiling a basket of cloth scraps, their colors rich against the weathered wood table. Spools of ribbon sat nearby, some faded, others still vibrant.

Her little brother Ian struggled with a knot until her Dad leaned down, his large hands guiding his son's smaller ones through the motion.

"Not too tight," he murmured. "Just enough to hold."

"Look what I made!" Ruth held up a milkweed pod painted gold with tiny red berries glued inside. Her face beamed with pride as Mom fastened a loop of twine to the top.

"That's beautiful," Mom said, ruffling his hair. "It'll catch the candlelight perfectly."

Merryn struggled with a slice of dried orange, her little fingers trying to thread a needle. Aunt Ellie knelt beside her, steadying her hand.

"Like this, sweetheart. Just push through—there you go."

Across the table, Quinn and Gemma worked on more elaborate designs, wrapping colorful cloth scraps around pinecones to create tiny woodland figures. The older children helped the younger ones, passing scissors and sharing ribbons with surprising patience. Marisol carefully painted a snowman on a slice of wood. Rosa bobbed up and down beside her trying to pick a color to paint the scarf.

As darkness fell outside, Gran appeared in the doorway, Pop beside her, carrying a wooden crate with careful reverence.

"Time for the old treasures," Gran announced, her voice softer than usual.

The box was placed on the cleared end of the table, and the family gathered around. Pop lifted the lid to reveal tissue-wrapped bundles nestled inside like sleeping birds.

"These survived in the attic," he explained. "Thought we'd never see them all up again, but here we are."

The box had very old ornaments, handmade ornaments, and other bits of Callahan history. Every year, a few hung on the tree among the new shiny ornaments, the blinking lights, and the tinsel. This year, Gran said,

"Even though we have those shiny ornaments and maybe even a box of tinsel in the attic, we felt this year we should go a hundred percent old school. Nature-made or hand-made."

Aunt Beth reached in first, unwrapping a small glass ball painted with delicate snowflakes. Her eyes glistened. "My first Christmas with Uncle Boone. Remember how the power went out then, too, just for the night?"

"And now look at us," Uncle Boone said, arm around her waist.

One by one, ornaments emerged from their paper nests. A silver star from Uncle Cole and Aunt Ellie's wedding. A tiny red boot Gran's mother had given her. A wooden train Pop had carved for her Dad's fifth Christmas.

"This one," Uncle Cole held up a clay snowman with the nose missing, "was the year I broke my arm falling from the apple tree."

"And I made this," Aunt Judith laughed through unexpected tears, lifting a cotton ball snowman with googly eyes, "the Christmas I was pregnant with Merryn."

Lily watched the adults' faces transform as they handled each delicate memory. Their expressions shifted between joy and grief, as though remembering not just Christmases past, but the world that had disappeared with them.

"This was yours, Boone," Pop said, passing a small wooden horse to his son. "Your grandfather carved it the year you were born."

"This one," Aunt Clare said, voice catching as she lifted a small ceramic angel, "was from Dad's mother. She gave it to us the last Christmas before she passed."

Tobias squeezed her shoulder as she wiped her eyes.

The room filled with stories; tales of holidays long past, family legends, embarrassing memories that brought howls of laughter. The children listened wide-eyed, connecting to a world they'd barely known. Their found family was enjoying the stories as well, and they added fun stories of their own Christmases past.

Lily hung a few special pieces, then retreated to a quiet corner with Beast stretched beside her. She pet his broad, black head, then opened her journal, pen poised. Across the room, Fiona lay against Fergus's warm bulk, colored chalks moving across paper as she captured the scene.

Their eyes met briefly, and Lily knew her cousin understood; they were the chroniclers of this historical moment, the first Christmas of their new world.

Lily wrote slowly:

Tonight I watched our family remember. Maybe that's what Christmas is really about now, not presents or lights, but keeping the good parts of the world before, so they don't disappear forever.

Her Dad began to strum his guitar, the familiar chords of "Silent Night" emerging soft and tentative. His gentle voice floated over the family, a baritone thread that wove through the room.

"O Holy Night..."

Gran joined first, her voice weathered but true. Then Uncle Boone and Uncle Cole's deeper tones, and Mom's clear soprano. Father Tom joined in on the piano and added his clear tenor voice to the rest. One by one, they all fell in, their voices merging into something greater than themselves.

Lily closed her notebook and sang too, watching as the music pulled everyone from their chairs. The carols fell over them like a prayer of hope and survival, connecting them to all the Christmases that had come before and all that might follow.

"Let's get the rest of these treasures where they belong," Gran said when the song ended.

The family gathered around the massive tree. Ruth handed ornaments to Ian so he could reach the lower branches. Uncle Cole helped the twins decorate the higher spots. Each ornament found its place, a constellation of memories illuminated by the fire's glow.

When only the star remained, Pop beckoned to Lucy. "Come here, little one."

He lifted her high above his shoulders, her small body stretching toward the treetop, the star clutched in her tiny hands.

"Steady now," he murmured as she placed it with solemn care.

* * *

The days after the tree-decorating blurred together in a happy frenzy of preparation. Mornings brought the scent of baking, afternoons were spent crafting, and evenings filled the lodge with laughter. Lily noticed how everyone seemed lighter, as though the holiday pushed grief to the edges for a while.

On the fourth afternoon, Aunt Jillian bustled through the door, her arms loaded with packages, cheeks flushed from the cold.

"Look what I found!" she called, unwrapping a bundle with careful hands. "I was going through Audrey's trunk, and..." Her voice caught slightly before she continued.

She laid several small quilted squares on the table, each one uniquely patterned, with neat pockets and ribbon ties.

"Mini gift-wrap quilts," Gran whispered, running her finger along the stitching. "Audrey was making these all year."

"She saved every scrap," Aunt Jillian said. "Said Christmas shouldn't create waste, not anymore… but it needs the fun of gift wrap and opening gifts."

Lily watched as hands reached out to touch the colorful squares. Each person's expression mirrored the same bittersweet mixture: joy in Audrey's thoughtfulness, sorrow in her loss, and the absence of her light.

"She always thought of everything," Aunt Beth said softly.

Across the room, Lily noticed Zeke staring at the quilts, his weathered face suddenly vulnerable. Gran saw it too, crossing to place her hand on his arm.

"First Christmas is the hardest," she murmured. "Emma Jean would've loved these."

Zeke nodded, his Adam's apple bobbing. "She'd say they're prettier than a peach orchard in springtime," he managed, attempting a smile.

Aunt Jillian, nearby, wiped her eyes quickly when she thought no one was looking. Her husband, Miguel's, absence seemed to hang in the space beside her.

The evening became their sanctuary from grief. After dinner, they gathered in the great room where children sprawled on the floor, stringing popcorn and cranberries into garlands. Dad taught Ian to thread the needle through each kernel without breaking it.

Some nights they played charades, Pictionary, or card games, filling the lodge with competitive shouts and laughter. Other evenings, Pop, Zeke, or Buck spun tales of Christmases from the world before, their deep voices painting pictures of glittering city lights and midnight services.

And always, there were the whispered secrets. Lily caught glimpses of projects quickly hidden when someone walked by, and heard hushed conversations stop abruptly when she entered rooms. She had her own secrets too, gifts crafted in stolen moments, wrapped in Audrey's quilted squares and tucked beneath her bed.

Each evening, she would take some time to write about everything she experienced. She described the taste of the food, the feelings that welled up at unexpected and random times, and the look of all of the beautiful decorations. She even copied down one of the evening stories Pop, Zeke, and Buck told.

* * *

Christmas, back in the day

by Lily Callahan

The fire crackled high in the big stone hearth. All of us kids sprawled on the rag rug, cheeks pink from sledding. Mugs of cocoa steamed on the table. The grown-ups settled in with that easy comfort that comes from being full, warm, and among their own.

Zeke stretched his boots toward the fire, his old hat pushed back on his head. Pop sat nearby in his huge, plush chair, Fergus's head lay in his lap, and Buck, the wiry old mountain man with a beard that could've hidden a small animal, lounged cross-legged on the floor, a Main Coon cat, Gypsy, asleep curled in his lap.

It didn't take much to get the three men started, just one of the grandkids asking what Christmas was like when *they* were young. This time, I asked what Christmas was like when they were little because I wanted to write it all down. Pop gave me that twinkly look he gets, the one that means a story's about to happen.

That was all it took.

Zeke rubbed his chin. "Well now, lemme tell ya. Y'all don't know how easy you got it these days. I remember one Christmas, Mama wrapped up a potato and told me it was a *training rock* for when I got big enough to have a slingshot."

The room laughed hard at this, but Buck snorted. "A potato, huh? Ain't you fancy! We couldn't afford potatoes. Mama gave me a lump of dirt and said, 'Use your imagination, boy.'"

Pop leaned forward, grinning ear to ear. "Ha! You fellas had it made. We were so poor one year, Daddy cut the bottom off his

16

long johns, rubbed 'em with pine needles, and said, 'There's your Christmas stocking, son.'"

The kids erupted in laughter. The littlest one, Merryn, squealed, "That's *gross!*"

Zeke wagged a finger. "Don't knock it, sweetheart. At least pine needles smell better than most of Pop's socks."

Buck chuckled. "He's got a point. We didn't even have a tree, y'know. We'd decorate a broom handle stuck in a flour sack. Mama'd hang dried beans on it and call it festive."

"Beans!" Pop wheezed with laughter. "We couldn't waste beans! We just drew a Christmas tree in the dirt floor with a stick, and we'd stare at it and hum carols till we fell asleep hungry."

Zeke smirked. "I do declare, Gus, your childhood sounds like a survival story written by a turnip."

The laughter built, spreading around the fire like warmth itself.

Buck took a sip of cider and leaned in. "You boys ever get toys?"

Zeke puffed up. "Sure—once. Daddy whittled me a wooden horse. Didn't have no legs, but I loved it anyhow. Rode that thing all winter."

Pop wagged his pipe. "Wooden horse? You were spoiled! I got a stick with a string tied to it. Called it *Stickey the Wonder Dog.* Took him for walks every day."

Buck nodded solemnly. "I had to *pretend* I had a stick. Couldn't afford the real thing."

"A pretend stick?" Pop said. "Now that's just sad. Pathetic really"

"Yep," Buck replied. "Named it Imaginary George. Best dog I ever didn't have."

That one sent the kids rolling.

The laughter faded into warm chuckles as Pop poked the fire. "You know, we make fun, but truth is, we didn't have much back then. I remember one Christmas it rained so hard the creek flooded the yard. Daddy just looked out and said, 'Well, at least Santa won't need to land…he can *dock*.'"

Zeke chuckled. "I got a single peppermint stick one year and thought I'd won the lottery."

Buck nodded. "I got a slice of apple and half a walnut. Ate 'em so slow I made it last three days."

Pop leaned back, a smile softening the lines of his face. "We sure were poor, but I don't ever remember feelin' it, not on Christmas."

"Me neither," Zeke said. "We had family, fire, and food—usually beans, but still food."

"And stories," Buck added. "Every year we'd sit by the fire, just like this, and try to one-up each other with tales 'bout who had it rougher. I reckon I've been playin' that same game for sixty years in one shape or another."

The other two men nodded, far away looks on their faces. It made Lily wonder what they were thinking.

For a second, nobody said anything. The fire popped. The wind outside made the windows rattle. It felt cozy and safe, like the kind of moment you don't realize is special until later.

Then I asked, "Did Santa ever come to your house, Pop?"

He smiled slowly. "Well, he tried. But by the time he got to our holler, he was so broke from feedin' them reindeer, he just left me a note that said, *IOU one Christmas. Signed, Santa.*"

Everyone cracked up again. Even Gran laughed so hard she had to wipe her eyes.

Pop leaned over and winked at me. "He finally paid me back tonight, sweetheart…'cause I got all of you here."

CHAPTER 2: FIONA

Fiona sat tucked into the corner of the room as Pop, Buck, and Zeke spun their tall tales. Her fingers moved across the paper with quiet purpose, capturing Pop's twinkling eyes, the way they crinkled at the corners when he was trying not to laugh at his own joke. She sketched Zeke's smile-creased face, all those lines that made him look like an old apple left in the sun too long, but in a good way. She added white to Buck's wild beard that stuck out in all directions like it had its own ideas about where to grow. The laughter from the latest outrageous claim; something about Pop's imaginary pet rock, provided perfect cover for her quiet observations. Fiona's tongue poked out between her teeth as she concentrated on getting the crinkles around Zeke's eyes just right.

The firelight made everything golden and shadowy at the same time. Perfect for drawing. She added silvery-white streaks to Gran's auburn hair and blue to Aunt Ellie's eyes. Gran's hands, slightly gnarled but gentle, rested on her cane. Fiona tried to draw the swollen knuckles just right—not to make them look ugly but to show how strong they were.

Her favorite thing was the box of multi-colored gift-wrapping quilts; they were fun to draw with all the assorted colors. Aunt Audrey's squares looked like little jewels when Lily held them up to admire in the candlelight, and Fiona had tried to capture that sparkle of metallic thread in her sketch.

Fiona flipped back through a few pages in her sketchbook. She smiled at her drawings of the big snowball fight, how Quinn had fallen backwards with his arms spread wide, and how Declan had managed to hit Dad right in the face. She'd drawn the tree cutting too; all the men pulling together on the rope while the great pine swayed. She laughed at her picture of the baking day, the flour streaks on everyone's face making them look like ghosts in Gran's kitchen.

These pages felt important. She felt her drawings were what they had for memories now. There were no more cameras or cell phones to take pictures anymore. No Instagram or Facebook to share what happened. Just her pencils and the paper Gran had given her for her birthday.

Now, memories lived in sketchbooks and journals, in songs sung around fires and stories told over and over until they became almost mythical. Sometimes she worried about forgetting how things looked, how moments felt. She always loved shapes and color, almost as much as Lily loved words.

She turned to a fresh page and began sketching the whole room; the fire throwing shadows, the circle of family, the laughter hanging in the air almost visible. She tried to draw that too. Not just the people, but the feeling of being together. The warmth that had nothing to do with the fire.

Years from now, when this moment was just a memory, she'd have this drawing to remind her how it felt to be surrounded by family, warm and safe while winter howled outside.

"Whatcha drawin' there, little bit?" Buck asked, peering over.

Fiona held up her sketchbook. "Us," she said simply. "So we remember."

＊ ＊ ＊

The next day, Fiona had crayons and paper spread across the big oak table. Her fingers guided Lucy's small, pudgy hand as they traced a wobbly Christmas tree together.

"More green," Lucy insisted, grabbing for the crayon with chubby fingers.

"Here you go," Fiona smiled, handing over the stubby green crayon that had seen better days.

Lucy beamed. "More sparkles?"

"Definitely more sparkles," Fiona nodded, sliding the jar of glitter closer while keeping it just out of baby Luke's reach.

Merryn's nose scrunched up in concentration as she carefully drew what might have been a reindeer or possibly a very lumpy dog. Even baby Luke participated, happily smacking his hands against a sheet of paper where Fiona had pressed his tiny palms into red paint to make a heart. Rosa and Jake squeezed in at the edges of the table, Rosa's dark curls falling forward as she meticulously drew snow-covered pines while Jake's Christmas tree ornaments looked suspiciously like baseballs.

The creative chaos spread across the room. Near the window, Marisol, Sadie, and Leah huddled together with balls of yarn in their laps, fingers working awkwardly with crochet hooks. Sadie let out a frustrated sigh as she unraveled another misshapen row.

"I'm never going to finish this scarf," she groaned.

"You'll get it," Marisol encouraged, though her own project looked equally questionable.

Sadie muttered something under her breath as she pulled out a row of crochet stitches for the third time.

"It's supposed to be a hat, not a pot holder," Sadie whispered.

Leah nodded sympathetically. "I messed up my first five rows too. Here, let me show you again."

By the hearth, Quinn and Edwin sat cross-legged on the floor, each holding small wooden objects and sandpaper. Wood shavings collected around them like sawdust snow. The firelight caught on the fine particles floating in the air around them.

"I'm thinking I'll try a fox next," Edwin said, turning a small wooden block in his hands, testing its smoothness. He was making blocks for Lucy.

"Too hard when you are just starting," Quinn replied, focused on his own creation. "Start with something simple, like a rabbit."

"If you angle the knife this way," Quinn demonstrated with an invisible blade, "you get cleaner edges on the ears." Edwin watched carefully and nodded.

Fiona glanced up from the table, her artist's eye drawn to the quiet scene across the room. Lily sat on the couch next to Gran, both bent over notebooks, pens moving steadily across pages. Their postures mirrored each other perfectly—heads tilted at the same angle, one ankle crossed over the other, occasional pauses to stare thoughtfully at the ceiling before writing again. Gran occasionally reached up to tuck a strand of auburn-and-silver hair behind her ear, and moments later, Lily did exactly the same with her own dark locks.

Fiona made a mental note of every detail; the afternoon light touching Gran's silver strands, the matching furrow of concentration between their brows, the way their hands moved across the page with the same rhythm. She would capture this later, preserve this moment of two generations of storytellers, side by side.

The peaceful scene erupted into chaos as Aunt Clare emerged from the kitchen carrying a plate piled high with cookies…sugar cookies shaped like stars, oatmeal with dried berries, and honey-nut rounds. The reaction was immediate and thunderous.

"Who's hungry?" she called, immediately surrounded by a stampede of children and men materializing from seemingly nowhere, hands outstretched and eyes gleaming with anticipation.

Fiona grabbed a sugar cookie and moved closer to the fire. She sat cross-legged on the braided rug near the fire, her sketchbook balanced on her knees. Beast snuggled up against her with a sigh. Her colored pencils moved fast and light, whispering against the page. She liked to draw quickly, before the moment changed or she could overthink it.

Zeke was laughing so hard his eyes were nearly closed, his shoulders shaking while Buck tried to keep his pipe lit and failed for the third time. Pop had his head thrown back, his white hair catching the firelight, and one of the dogs was asleep against his leg. Max, Jake, and Ian were piled together on the couch, fighting over a blanket, and Gran sat in her rocker, watching it all with that look—the kind that's half amusement, half peace.

Fiona didn't need to look up to draw them anymore. She could feel the shapes, the movement, the glow. She made soft lines for Grandma's hands folded in her lap, bold strokes for Pop's laughter, tiny curls of smoke from Buck's stubborn pipe.

Her pencil paused, then she added the fire; thick, orange scribbles that bled into the edges of the family circle. To her, the fire wasn't just light. It was *love*. It reached out and touched everyone.

When she finally stopped, the room was quieter. Someone was humming "Silent Night," and snow brushed against the window. Fiona looked down at her drawing. It wasn't perfect, Pop's face was a little lopsided, and the dog looked like a loaf of bread, but it was real.

It looked like *home*.

"Whatcha got there, little Miss?" Buck leaned over, his beard nearly touching her sketchbook.

Fiona hesitated, suddenly shy. Her drawings were like her secrets, the way she saw the world when no one was looking.

"It's just everyone," she mumbled, fingers tracing the edge of her paper.

"May I?" Buck reached out with rough hands that could build a cabin but now moved with unexpected gentleness.

Fiona handed him the drawing. The room fell quiet as Buck held it up, his weathered face softening.

"Well, I'll be," he whispered. "You've caught the light, little one. You've caught the very heart of it."

Pop rose from his chair, crossing to Buck's side. His large hand settled on Fiona's shoulder as he studied the drawing.

"You've got magic in those fingers, granddaughter," Pop said, voice gruff with emotion. "Just like your Gran with her words."

From her rocker, Gran smiled. "Storytellers come in all forms. Some use words, some use pictures. Both keep memories alive."

Fiona felt warmth bloom inside her chest, brighter than any fire. In a world without cameras or phones or screens, her drawings were becoming something more than just pictures. They were becoming the family's memories, preserved on paper.

"Will you draw another?" little Rosa asked, eyes wide with wonder.

Fiona flipped to a clean page, pencil poised. This time, she'd capture Rosa's hopeful face, the cookie crumbs on her chin, the way the firelight danced in her dark eyes.

Fiona thought, *If I could draw happiness, this would be it.*

* * *

Lily and Fiona sat in the sunny kitchen window whispering excitedly. Beth walked in from the henhouse with a basket of eggs, and her eyes narrowed when she saw the girls.

"What are you two whispering about?" Beth asked as she set the basket on the counter and headed over to the girls. Lily turned sideways and dropped a dishtowel over the items on the window seat between them.

"Nothing." They replied in unison.

"Mmmm Hmmm," Beth said as she raised her eyebrow.

"Mooooooooom, it's Christmas stuff. You can't look." Fiona said.

"It is a good secret, Aunt Beth, it really is," Lily said with a crooked smile.

Beth nodded and picked the basket back up and headed to the root cellar.

Jake and Max came crashing through the kitchen, followed closely by a furious-looking Sadie and Leah. Gran stepped out of the kitchen's cooking area to the main counter and smacked a wooden spoon down with a loud whack!

"Calm it down or take it outside!" Gran hollered, her voice carrying the authority that could silence even Pop when needed.

The boys skidded to a halt, socked feet sliding across the worn wooden floor. Sadie, her face flushed with anger, nearly collided with Max's back.

"But they stole our ribbons!" Leah gestured wildly at the boys. "The ones we were saving for—"

"For nothing," Sadie cut in, giving her cousin a sharp look. "Just stuff."

24

Lily and Fiona exchanged knowing glances. Everyone had secrets this week.

"Did not steal," Jake protested, hands raised defensively. "We borrowed. For a project."

"A Christmas project," Max added, bouncing on his toes.

Gran lowered the wooden spoon but kept it poised like a weapon. "Then you ask permission first. That's how borrowing works."

The kitchen door swung open again as Franklin entered, his arms full of split wood. "What's the commotion in here? Heard Gran's spoon-slam from the woodpile."

"The annual Christmas conspiracy has begun," Gran said dryly, but her eyes sparkled. She turned back to the children. "Everybody working on surprises, are we?"

Five heads nodded solemnly.

"Then we need a system," Gran declared. "Corner by the pantry is for the boys. Window seat for the girls. Anyone caught snooping loses cookie privileges."

"For how long?" Jake asked, horrified.

"Forever," Gran said with a straight face.

The children's eyes widened before they caught the twitch at the corner of her mouth. Lily bit her lip to keep from laughing as Fiona carefully tucked their project deeper under the dishtowel.

Gran turned toward Lily and Fiona, her stern expression softening into a conspiratorial smile.

"Now, what are you two crafting over there that's so secret?"

"It's a huge secret. Gran, where can we finish it so that nobody will bother us?" Fiona asked.

"We keep getting interrupted, we are never going to finish!" Lily added dramatically.

Gran laughed and said, "Just this one time….you girls can go work at my desk in my room."

The girls squealed with excitement and began gathering their supplies.

Franklin stacked the wood in the box by the stove. "Remember when Christmas was store-bought surprises instead of stolen ribbon wars?"

"This is better," Lily said softly, meeting her father's eyes.

* * *

Gran tapped lightly on her bedroom door. "Girls, are you coming down for lunch?"

"No, Gran…we are just too busy right now," Fiona called from behind the door.

"I figured as much. I'm putting a tray of sandwiches and fruit out here," she said, placing the food on the floor outside the door.

Fiona looked at her cousin and grinned. She wiped her chalk-colored hands on her pants and went to grab the tray from the hallway. She returned with a beach towel over her arm and a tray piled with sandwiches, canned fruit mix, potato chips, and iced tea. Lily grabbed the towel and spread it on the floor, then they sat down to a picnic lunch, discussing the project in detail.

"How long do you think we should make it?" Fiona asked between bites of her sandwich.

She looked at her cousin and saw that Lily was thinking hard about it. Finally, she just shrugged.

"I'm not sure. How many pictures do you have? Let's see how many of my stories match your pictures." Lily suggested.

Fiona crawled over to Gran's bed where they'd spread out dozens of sketches. Her fingers, still stained with colored chalk, hovered over the drawings, careful not to smudge them.

"I've got almost everyone. Look, here's Pop telling stories with Zeke and Buck. And Gran teaching you to make jam." She shuffled through more drawings. "The boys building that snow fort. Aunt Mary painting Christmas scenes on scrap wood."

Lily popped a potato chip in her mouth and leaned over the artwork. "These are perfect. Your drawings show exactly what I wrote about in my journal." She reached for her notebook, flipping through pages filled with her neat handwriting.

"We could organize them by family? Or maybe by days?" Lily suggested, matching a story about Uncle Boone's failed attempt at ice fishing with Fiona's sketch of her father slipping into shallow water.

Fiona shook her head, a loose strand of hair falling across her face. "What about organizing it like the seasons? Starting with the tree cutting, then all the preparation stuff, and ending with…"

"Christmas Eve!" they exclaimed together, then dissolved into giggles.

"Gran's going to cry," Lily whispered, suddenly serious.

Fiona nodded, placing the sketch of Gran reading by the fire on top. "The good kind of crying, though. All the moms might cry."

They munched on their sandwiches in companionable silence, the winter light streaming through the window casting long shadows across the floor. Outside, they could hear the distant shouts of their cousins sledding down the hill behind the lodge.

"This is going to be the best Christmas present ever," Fiona said softly.

* * *

Lily appeared in the kitchen shortly before dinner with dirty dishes. Mary was at the sink and took the dishes from her daughter with a curious smile. "Are you two sneaky girls all done?"

Lily shook her head as she took two sticks of jerky and headed back toward the stairs.

"You two will be down for dinner. No arguments. So start finishing up and getting Gran and Pop's room back in order." her mother called after her.

Lily waved a hand over her head in acknowledgement as she disappeared up the stairs.

Fiona sat at her Gran's desk, chalk dust powdering her hands, sleeves, and the desk top. She was working on a drawing of the main room, looking down from the top of the stairs, at the tree and the colorfully wrapped gifts, the warm glow of the fire. Her Pop in his big chair, glasses perched on his nose, reading and absently petting Fergus's head. Gran crocheting with Odin's head in her lap. She could see it clearly in her mind. This was the first thing they will all see when they looked at their gift. It had to be perfect. Lily came in and leaned over Fiona's shoulder to see her progress. Handing her a stick of jerky, Lily said, "Oh my Fi! This is the best picture you have ever drawn."

Fiona didn't look up, her tongue caught between her teeth as she smudged shadows beneath the Christmas tree with her pinky finger. The chalk dust rose in a tiny cloud.

"You really think so?" she murmured, tilting her head to examine her work. "I want it to look exactly like it feels when you're standing up there looking down. Like everything's safe and golden."

Lily squeezed her shoulder. "It does. You can practically feel the heat from the fire."

Fiona finally sat back, wiping her chalky hands on her already stained jeans. She took the jerky from Lily and chewed thoughtfully, studying the drawing.

"Mom says we need to clean up and be down for dinner soon." Lily began gathering loose papers and organizing them into neat stacks. "And we need to put Gran and Pop's room back how we found it."

Fiona nodded, still focused on her masterpiece. "Just let me finish the light on Pop's glasses. And maybe a little more shadow under Odin."

The evening light was fading fast outside the window, casting the room in a soft blue glow. Fiona worked quickly now, adding final touches while Lily tidied around her. The jerky hung from her mouth as both hands worked the chalk.

"Time's up, Fi," Lily said, opening Gran's closet to return the extra blankets they'd spread out for their workspace.

Fiona signed her name in tiny letters at the bottom corner of the drawing, then carefully set it aside to be sprayed with fixative. She stood and stretched her cramped fingers, leaving dusty chalk prints on her shirt.

"This is going to be worth all the secrecy," she whispered, glancing at their nearly completed project. "I can't wait to see their faces."

Fiona smiled, "I want them to feel it when they look at it. The quiet. The warmth."

"We should start cleaning up." Lily glanced around at the artistic chaos they'd created in Gran and Pop's room. "Mom said dinner's soon."

She sat back, jerky forgotten in her hand, and studied her work. For the first time in her young artistic life, what she saw on paper matched what she'd imagined in her mind. The lodge's heart… captured in chalk and paper.

"It's perfect," Lily whispered to Fiona, as if speaking too loudly might disturb the scene she'd created.

CHAPTER 3: LILY

Lily and Fiona lay in bed that night with the blanket over their heads, whispering. Lily read a page of her notebook to Fiona in a hushed voice.

"Oh my Lily, you do have a way with words. It is like stepping into a memory when you read that. I can see the scene in my head, just like my pictures. That section must be part of our gift." Fiona said, clapping her hands.

"We only have two more days. Do you think we will be done?" Lily asked in a worried whisper.

"Yes, because we will make this one Christmas, but we will make others too. Maybe one for each season or each holiday? We will be apocalypse correspondents, or maybe 'the memory keepers', or, or, or..." Fiona rambled excitedly

"I get it! Jeez, relax. If we just keep it to this Christmas we can get it done and work on other books later. That is brilliant. Maybe we should go back in time and start at the beginning of the end." Lily laughed. She was getting excited too. Her fingers itched to write down every single thing. Instead she looked through her journal and pulled out interesting, touching, or funny events and re-wrote them as short stories.

Suddenly Gemma yanked the blankets off of their heads.

"Will you two shut it and go to sleep?" she whispered sharply. Gemma mumbled under her breath as she headed back to bed.

Fiona bit her lip to stifle a giggle while Lily rolled her eyes at their cousin's retreating form. The moonlight filtering through the window cast long shadows across their shared room, illuminating the scattered pages of Lily's journal and Fiona's sketches.

"Sorry," Fiona whispered, her voice barely audible.

Lily pulled the blanket back over them, creating their secret tent once more. "We should sleep anyway. Tomorrow we need to finish binding everything together."

"I can't sleep. I keep thinking about Gran's face when she opens it." Fiona's eyes gleamed in the darkness of their makeshift fort. "Gran is gonna cry?"

"Definitely." Lily nodded solemnly.

From across the room, they heard Gemma's irritated sigh followed by the creak of her bed as she turned over.

Lily pressed a finger to her lips and carefully folded her journal closed. They would have to wait until morning to continue their secret project. But as they settled into their pillows, both girls' minds raced with ideas—stories waiting to be written, moments waiting to be drawn.

"Memory keepers," Lily whispered, testing the words. "I like that. Gran says you can tell stories with pictures and with words and I think she is right."

Fiona smiled in the darkness, already half-dreaming of more scenes to capture, more memories to preserve in chalk and charcoal. Because in this new world, without phones or cameras or computers, someone needed to remember everything exactly as it was.

Someone needed to keep the memories alive.

* * *

Christmas Eve draped the lodge in a chaotic blanket of excitement. Lily sat cross-legged on the hearth, journal open on her lap, watching the day unfold like a play. The scent of pine and cinnamon hung in the air as voices echoed through every room. She scribbled furiously, determined to capture each moment before it slipped away.

In the living room, Dad and Uncle Boone stood with identical expressions of mock despair as they realized something vital was missing from the festivities.

"How can we have Christmas with no taffy?" Franklin asked with an exaggerated whine, his hands gesturing wildly at the spread of treats on the sideboard.

"Yeah Ma, it is a tradition!" Boone cried as he fell back dramatically onto the couch, the back of his hand across his forehead. The ancient springs creaked under his weight, and several children giggled at his performance.

Lily laughed, quickly jotting down their dramatics in her notebook. She'd never seen grown men so upset about candy before.

Gran looked up from her knitting, one eyebrow raised. "And whose job was it to make the taffy this year?"

Uncle Boone and Dad exchanged glances, suddenly finding the ceiling and floor incredibly interesting.

"That's what I thought," Gran said with a triumphant smile. "Maybe next year you two will remember instead of assuming the taffy fairy will magically appear."

Pop wandered in from the kitchen, munching on a cookie. "What's all the fuss about?"

"The boys are having a crisis because there's no Christmas taffy," Mary explained, winking at Lily.

"No taffy?" Pop looked genuinely stricken. "Well, that just won't do."

Lily closed her journal, tucking her pencil behind her ear. This was getting interesting. The men of the Callahan family took their Christmas sweets very seriously…a detail she definitely needed to include in her and Fiona's gift.

"If only we had sugar and butter and strong arms to pull it," Gran mused innocently, her knitting needles clicking away.

Dad and Uncle Boone perked up immediately.

"We still have time!" Dad announced.

"Kitchen. Now. You to Pop." Uncle Boone pointed dramatically toward the kitchen.

Lily scrambled to her feet, not wanting to miss a moment of this. Christmas Eve was proving to be the perfect final chapter for their memory book.

Lily grabbed Fiona's arm as she walked by and the two followed the men to the kitchen. They slipped through the doorway just in time to see her Dad pulling out every pot and pan he could find while Uncle Boone rummaged through the pantry.

"Do you even know how to make taffy?" Fiona whispered, her eyes wide as she took in the spectacle.

Lily shook her head. "I don't think they do either."

Pop stood at the counter, sleeves already rolled up, a look of determination on his weathered face as he studied an ancient recipe card. "Two cups of sugar, one cup of water—where's the cream of tartar?"

"The what now?" Uncle Boone's voice echoed from inside the pantry.

"Mama are you sure letting those men loose in the kitchen?" Aunt Clare asked with her eyebrows raised, appearing in the doorway behind the girls.

Uncle Tobias squeezed past them, followed closely by Uncle Owen. "I helped my grandmother make taffy once," Tobias announced confidently.

"When you were what—ten?" Uncle Owen smirked.

"Not sure this is the best idea..." Aunt Judith added as she peered into the increasingly crowded kitchen where a metal bowl clattered to the floor.

Father Tom had a grin from ear to ear as he watched the chaos while he bounced Lucy on his knee. The little girl giggled as he bounced her higher with each crash from the kitchen.

"I can go supervise if you want," he said with a chuckle.

"Absolutely not!" Gran said as she stood up and headed for the kitchen. "Adding another man to the bunch will help no one."

She paused in the doorway, taking in the scene—Franklin with sugar already dusting his beard, Boone arguing with Owen about proper butter temperature, and Pop squinting at the recipe card as if it were written in hieroglyphics.

"Lord give me strength," Gran muttered, then clapped her hands sharply. The noise startled everyone into silence. "Franklin, step away from that stove. Boone, put down that whisk before you hurt yourself."

Lily pulled her notebook out, frantically writing. This was gold. Pure Christmas Eve gold.

"But Jo, we just want to—" Pop began.

"I know exactly what you want, Augustus Callahan, but what I want is not to have you destroy my kitchen on Christmas Eve." Gran's voice was stern, but her eyes twinkled. "Now if you insist on making taffy, we'll do it properly. I will mix it and you gentlemen will do the pulling."

Gran's Molasses Pulled Taffy

Recorded by Lily Callahan

5 teaspoons butter, softened, divided
1/4 cup water
1-1/4 cups packed brown sugar
2 tablespoons cider vinegar
1/4 teaspoon salt

1/3 cup molasses

Butter a 15x10x1-in. pan with 3 teaspoons butter; set aside. In a heavy saucepan, combine the water, brown sugar, vinegar and salt. Bring to a boil over medium heat. Cook and stir until a candy thermometer reads 245° (firm-ball stage), stirring occasionally. Add molasses and remaining butter. Cook, uncovered until a candy thermometer reads 260° (hard-ball stage), stirring occasionally. Remove from the heat; pour into prepared pan. Cool for 5 minutes or until cool enough to handle. Pull and fold until the Taffy turns pale.

As evening approached, the chill of Christmas Eve retreated before the light of dozens of candles. Excitement buzzed through the air like electricity, setting even the adults on edge with anticipation. The massive pine tree dominated the great room, its branches heavy with handmade ornaments and strings of dried cranberries and popcorn, its base surrounded by packages wrapped in Audrey's colorful patchwork cloths.

Father Tom appeared at the door, bundled against the cold. "The chapel fire is lit. Mass begins in thirty minutes."

The group bundled up against the biting wind, forming a procession through the snowy path to the small chapel. Lanterns bobbed in the darkness, creating pools of golden light against the blue-white snow. Inside, the chapel glowed with warmth, its simple wooden cross adorned with pine boughs and red berries. Jo squeezed Gus's hand and nodded to Marcus as he reached his hand to steady Deb when she slipped. Deb caught his arm, looked up and smiled at Marcus. She held his arm the rest of the way, his hand resting on hers. Gus looked down at Jo and winked. Jo grinned and raised an eyebrow in Quinn's direction. He walked hand in hand with Grace, who had come from the school group to spend Christmas with him.

Gus squeezed her hand, a huge smile on his face.

Father Tom's voice rose and fell in the familiar rhythms of the Mass, bringing comfort in its continuity. His voice was comforting. The children sat unusually still, their faces solemn in the candlelight. When they sang "Silent Night," their voices blended in perfect harmony, echoing against the wooden walls.

Lily watched the flames dance across the weathered faces of her family, creating shadows that made everyone look mysterious and ancient. She had positioned herself between Fiona and Gran, her journal tucked safely in her coat pocket. Some moments needed to be lived first, written later, when the memory had settled into her heart.

Gran's voice rose clear and strong during "O Holy Night," her eyes closed as she sang the familiar words. Pop watched her with such tenderness that Lily had to look away, feeling as though she'd glimpsed something too private for her young eyes.

Father Tom stood before them, his face aglow in the candlelight. "Tonight we celebrate not just the birth of our Savior, but the miracle of light in darkness. This year has brought challenges none of us could have imagined. We've lost much…our comforts, our certainties, and loved ones."

His gaze swept across the gathered faces, lingering on those who had suffered the most painful losses.

"But look around you. We have not lost what matters most. Love. Faith. Community. Family, both born and found. These lights we hold—" he gestured to the candles, "—remind us that darkness cannot overcome light. Not even the smallest flame."

Lily felt a lump form in her throat as she glanced at her parents, at her siblings, at all the people who had become her world. Dad caught her eye and winked. Mom blew her a silent kiss. She watched as her younger siblings sang with gusto. Ian sat beside their mother, his small hand in hers. Ruth swayed her head to the Christmas carol. Her heart felt full, despite the hard year they had been through.

"In the days ahead," Father Tom continued, "remember that Christ came into a world of darkness and uncertainty not so different from our own. The shepherds had no electric lights, no running water, no modern conveniences. They had the stars above, the warmth of their fires, and each other."

When communion began, the family moved forward in groups, the older children helping the younger ones navigate the narrow aisle. Ian tripped on a loose floorboard, and Uncle Tobias caught him before he fell, lifting him easily onto his shoulders. The boy's giggles broke the solemnity, bringing smiles to tired faces.

As they filed out after Mass, the cold air hit them like a shock. The snow had stopped, and the sky had cleared, revealing a canopy of stars so brilliant they seemed close enough to touch. The children gasped, pointing upward in wonder.

"Look," Pop said, his breath forming clouds, "God's own Christmas lights."

The procession of lanterns wound its way back through the snow-laden path to the Lodge, where golden light spilled from every window. Stomping boots and peeling off layers filled the entryway with commotion as everyone hurried to escape the biting cold.

"I'm starving," Ian announced, his small voice carrying over the crowd.

"Good thing Gran's been cooking all day," Lily whispered to Fiona, who nodded eagerly.

They sat around the table as platter after platter came from the kitchen. Gasps rippled through the group. The massive oak table groaned under platters of venison, rabbit stew, and precious stored vegetables. Jo had used precious flour for rolls that filled the room with their yeasty aroma, and three pies cooled on the sideboard, a Christmas miracle of hoarded and improvised ingredients.

"How did you manage all this, Jo?" Marcus asked, his eyes wide at the feast before them.

Gran smiled mysteriously. "Christmas magic, and a lot of help from the ladies while you men were busy failing at taffy-pulling."

Everyone laughed as they found their places, the family filling every inch of available space. Pop stood at the head of the table, raising his cup. "To family, to light in darkness, and to hope that never dies."

"To hope," they echoed, the word hanging in the air like a prayer.

Father Tom blessed the meal and those gathered and then they dug in to the first real feast in a very long time.

Throughout the meal, young eyes darted repeatedly toward the waiting presents. Lucy could barely stay in her seat, while Jake's leg bounced constantly under the table. The smaller ones fidgeted and Max sighed repeatedly. Rosa and Ruth had the giggles. Even the teenagers showed signs of impatience.

"Those pies won't taste any sweeter if you keep looking at the tree instead of your plate," Pop teased, but his eyes sparkled with understanding.

Mary caught Franklin's eye across the table. "Remember how you used to sneak downstairs at midnight to shake all the packages?"

"I did not!" Franklin protested, but his reddening ears gave him away.

"Dad!" Lily cried in mock horror.

Beth reached over to ruffle Rowan's hair. "Like father, like daughter. I caught this one testing the weight of her gifts yesterday."

"Mom!" Rowan groaned, cheeks reddening.

Jo watched her family with quiet joy, her hand finding Gus's beneath the table. This Christmas might look different from all those that came before, but the heart of it remained unchanged – love, gathered around a table, impatient for the giving to begin.

* * *

Pop rose to his feet as the last bite of pie disappeared, tapping his glass for attention.

"When the kitchen is clean and everything is put away," he announced, his eyes twinkling, "we will meet in the main room, around the tree, and we will read 'Twas the Night Before Christmas' and each open one gift."

The words had barely left his lips before a flurry of activity erupted. Plates vanished from the table as small and large hands alike whisked them away. Lily found herself swept into the kitchen between Mary and Beth, a towel thrust into her hands as steaming water filled the basin. Forks and spoons clattered, plates stacked, and laughter filled the crowded space.

"Don't just rinse them, Jake! Scrub!" Gemma commanded, nudging her him aside to demonstrate proper technique.

"The faster we finish, the faster we get to presents," Sadie reminded everyone, her voice rising with excitement as she dried a serving platter.

At the sink, Lily worked methodically, passing clean dishes to Max who dried them with surprising care. Through the doorway, she could see Fiona organizing the younger children into a line, each carrying something light back to its proper place.

"Pop's sneaky," Donovan whispered to Lily as he passed behind her with an armload of leftovers. "He knows exactly how to make us clean up in record time."

"He sure does!" Laughed Declan as he nudged his brother to hurry him along.

In the dining room, Jo supervised as Ruth and Rosa carefully folded the tablecloth, while Quinn and Ian collected candle stubs for reuse. Outside the windows, night pressed close against the glass, but inside, the Lodge hummed with anticipation.

Aunt Clare appeared with a broom, sweeping crumbs into neat piles that Merryn scooped into a small bucket. "For the chickens tomorrow," she explained, taking her job very seriously.

Uncle Zeke and Buck rearranged the furniture in the main room, creating a half-circle around the tree and fireplace. The ornaments caught the flickering light, casting dancing shadows across the ceiling.

"Is this clean enough?" Lucy asked, holding up a questionable spoon for inspection.

"Try again, sweetheart," Beth said gently, guiding the toddler's small hands back into the water.

Twenty minutes of whirlwind activity accomplished what normally took an hour. Children lined up for inspection, hands thrust forward to prove they were clean and dry. Adults exchanged knowing glances, remembering their own childhood impatience.

Pop stood by the hearth, the large leatherbound book in his hands, watching as his family filed in and found seats. Jo lowered herself carefully into her rocking chair beside him, Odin settling at her feet. The firelight caught the silver in their hair, casting them both in a gentle glow.

"Well," Pop said, his voice soft with wonder, "that was the fastest cleanup in Callahan history."

Gus sat in his big chair beside the fire. He opened the old, leatherbound book, and perched his glasses on his nose. The grandchildren gathered at his feet, along with Odin, Beast, Fergus, Gypsy and two orange tabbies who had claimed the Lodge as their domain when the world changed. Fiona and Lily sat side by side, shoulders touching, sharing secret glances that spoke of their hidden project.

"Pop looks a lot like Santa right now." Fiona giggled, nudging her sister.

"Except he doesn't have a belly like a bowl full of jelly." Lily laughed, keeping her voice low but not quite low enough.

Pop cleared his throat dramatically and looked over his glasses to see if they were paying attention. His eyes, crinkled at the corners, swept across the sea of faces before him; children with flushed cheeks and bright eyes, adults with tired smiles that held both loss and gratitude.

The candlelight caught the silver of his beard as he winked at the girls. Around the room, the adults settled into their spots, Jo in her rocker, Mary curled against Franklin on the loveseat, Cole with an arm around Ellie. Clare passed mugs of hot cider while Tobias stoked the fire, sending sparks dancing up the chimney like fireflies. Then the two settle on the couch together.

Outside, snow fell silently against the windows, nature's lace curtains drawn across the glass. Inside, the Lodge held them all in its wooden embrace, sheltering them from the dark and cold.

Looking around at all of the expectant faces around him, Gus smiled and turned the page. The paper, yellowed with age, crackled beneath his weathered fingers. The room fell silent save for the popping of the fire and the occasional contented sigh of a child leaning against a parent's knee.

"'Twas the night before Christmas and all through the house, not a creature was stirring, not even a mouse..." he read in his deep, rich voice.

The familiar words washed over them like a blessing, a ritual unchanged despite everything else that had transformed in their world. Merryn's mouth formed the words silently, her eyes wide. Ian snuggled closer to Mary, his small hand clutching his father's pant leg. Even the teenagers, trying so hard to be grown, leaned forward slightly, caught in the spell of tradition and memory.

* * *

The last word of the poem hung in the air for a heartbeat before Pop snapped the book shut. His eyes twinkled with mischief, brighter than any electric Christmas light had ever been.

Then Gus clapped his hands together, breaking the trance, "One gift each!"

Chaos erupted immediately. Children scrambled toward the pile of packages wrapped in Audrey's mini quilts, brown paper, and bits of colorful fabric. Little feet thundered across the wooden floor as Max dove headfirst toward a lumpy package with his name scrawled on it. Jake and Edwin collided midway, tumbling into a laughing heap. The adults weren't much better, rising from their seats with barely contained excitement.

Boone put two fingers to his lips and whistled so loudly that Odin's ears perked up and the room froze. "Gran is going to pass out a gift to each person..." He gestured with both hands downward. "Everyone, sit down." He laughed as the children settled, cross-legged on the floor, vibrating with anticipation.

Jo stood with her cane, waving away Gus's offered hand. "I can manage perfectly well, thank you." Her voice was mock-stern, but her eyes danced with the same excitement as the children's. She made her way to the tree, where Mary had arranged the gifts in tidy piles.

"Let's see... who should go first?" Jo made a show of considering, tapping her finger against her lips while the younger children squirmed.

"Merryn," she decided, selecting a small package wrapped in a blue cloth tied with twine. "From your mama and daddy."

The little girl's face lit up as she carefully untied the twine instead of tearing into the package. Inside was a small wooden animal—a fox, intricately carved and polished to a shine.

"Daddy made it!" she breathed, holding it up for everyone to see.

"He sure did," Judith confirmed, smiling at Owen, who ducked his head modestly.

One by one, Jo called names and handed out gifts. Each recipient unwrapped their treasure while everyone watched, a shared ritual that stretched the joy further. Quinn received a new hunting knife with a bone handle, Sadie a knitted hat with matching mittens, Buck a carved pipe, and Mary a jar of precious infused honey.

"Ohhhhs" and "ahhhs" filled the room with each reveal, the simplicity of the gifts making them all the more precious. No electronic toys, no plastic packaging; just lovingly crafted items made by hands that cared.

Grace's hands trembled as she unwrapped the small, flat package from Quinn. When the cloth fell away to reveal a leather-bound sketchbook and a set of handmade charcoal pencils, her breath caught in her throat. Her eyes welled with tears as she ran her fingers over the smooth cover, memory and possibility flooding through her at once.

"I remembered you saying you used to draw... before." Quinn's voice was quiet, almost shy. "Thought maybe you might want to again. I asked Fi if she thought these pencils would work." He blushed a bit and shrugged.

She clutched the sketchbook to her chest, speechless. Six months ago, she'd been someone else entirely; a captive, a survivor, a ghost. Now she sat in this warm room, surrounded by people who'd taken her in without question when Quinn had found her wandering half-starved and bleeding in the forest. The gift wasn't just pencils and paper. It was recognition of who she'd been before everything had shattered, acknowledgment that those parts of her still existed somewhere inside.

"Thank you," she whispered, unable to find better words. The simple phrase felt impossibly inadequate, but Quinn's gentle smile told her he understood everything she couldn't say.

Across the room, Deb gasped softly as she opened a small cloth pouch. From it, she withdrew a delicate pendant hanging from a thin chain—a heart carved from bone, polished until it gleamed in the firelight, with a small "D" etched into its surface. Her eyes met Marcus's, filled with tears and question.

"Made it myself," the former Marine said gruffly, looking uncharacteristically uncertain. "Been carrying it around for weeks waiting for the right time."

Deb's fingers closed around the pendant as tears spilled down her cheeks. The room fell quiet, everyone pretending not to watch this unexpected moment between two people who'd been circling each other since Marcus arrived months ago.

Jo broke the spell, tapping her cane gently on the floor. "Alright, little ones. Bedtime. Santa won't come until you're asleep."

Father Tom had already scooped up Lucy, who had fallen asleep against his shoulder, her small face peaceful in the firelight. The other younger children groaned good-naturedly but rose to their feet, exchanging goodnights and thank-yous.

The older kids gathered the precious wrappings—Audrey's quilted squares and bits of fabric—carefully folding and placing them back into the wooden box where they'd be stored for next Christmas. Quinn sat with Grace, his hand in hers. The sketchbook still clutched tightly to her chest like a shield, or perhaps a promise.

* * *

Moonlight slipped through the curtains, casting silver ribbons across the floor of the crowded bedroom. The cabin had settled into that special kind of Christmas Eve quiet—the kind that vibrates with anticipation rather than true stillness.

Under a mound of quilts, Lily and Fiona huddled together, a flashlight between them casting a warm circle of light beneath their blanket tent. Their faces glowed as they examined their creation one final time.

"Do you think there's enough room for one more?" Fiona whispered, pencil poised over the final page. "I want to add Pop reading tonight."

Lily nodded, careful not to disturb the flashlight. "It's perfect. The beginning of the book is us getting the tree, and the end is tonight. Like a circle."

Fiona's hand moved with practiced confidence, sketching the outline of Pop in his chair, the book on his lap. She captured his reading glasses perched on the end of his nose, the way his eyebrows raised dramatically at the exciting parts. With a few deft strokes, she added the children gathered around, their faces upturned in wonder.

"You made everyone look so happy," Lily whispered.

"Because we are." Fiona blew gently on the page to set the pencil marks. "Even with everything that happened this year."

From across the room came Leah's soft snore, and both girls froze, stifling giggles. In the bed by the window, Gemma had finally fallen asleep, one arm flung dramatically across her face.

Lily carefully tied the ribbon around their completed book, the pages a beautiful blend of her careful handwriting and Fiona's expressive sketches. They'd titled it "The First Christmas After," and filled it with all the moments worth remembering—Gran's kitchen battle plans, Uncle Buck's wild stories, the tree decoration, even Odin stealing a sugar cookie when no one was looking.

"Gran's going to cry so hard," Fiona predicted as Lily wrapped the book in a square of Audrey's Christmas quilt fabric.

"Good crying though," Lily murmured, tucking the package safely under her pillow. "I hope she knows how much we love her. I hope they all do."

The day's excitement finally began to catch up with them. Fiona yawned, her eyes growing heavy as she switched off the flashlight. Lily pulled the blankets up to their chins as they settled back against their pillows.

"Merry Christmas," Fiona whispered, her voice already thick with approaching sleep.

"Merry Christmas," Lily replied, but her cousin was already drifting away, breathing deep and even.

Outside, the first new snowflakes of Christmas morning began to fall, silent and perfect, covering the world in fresh white possibility.

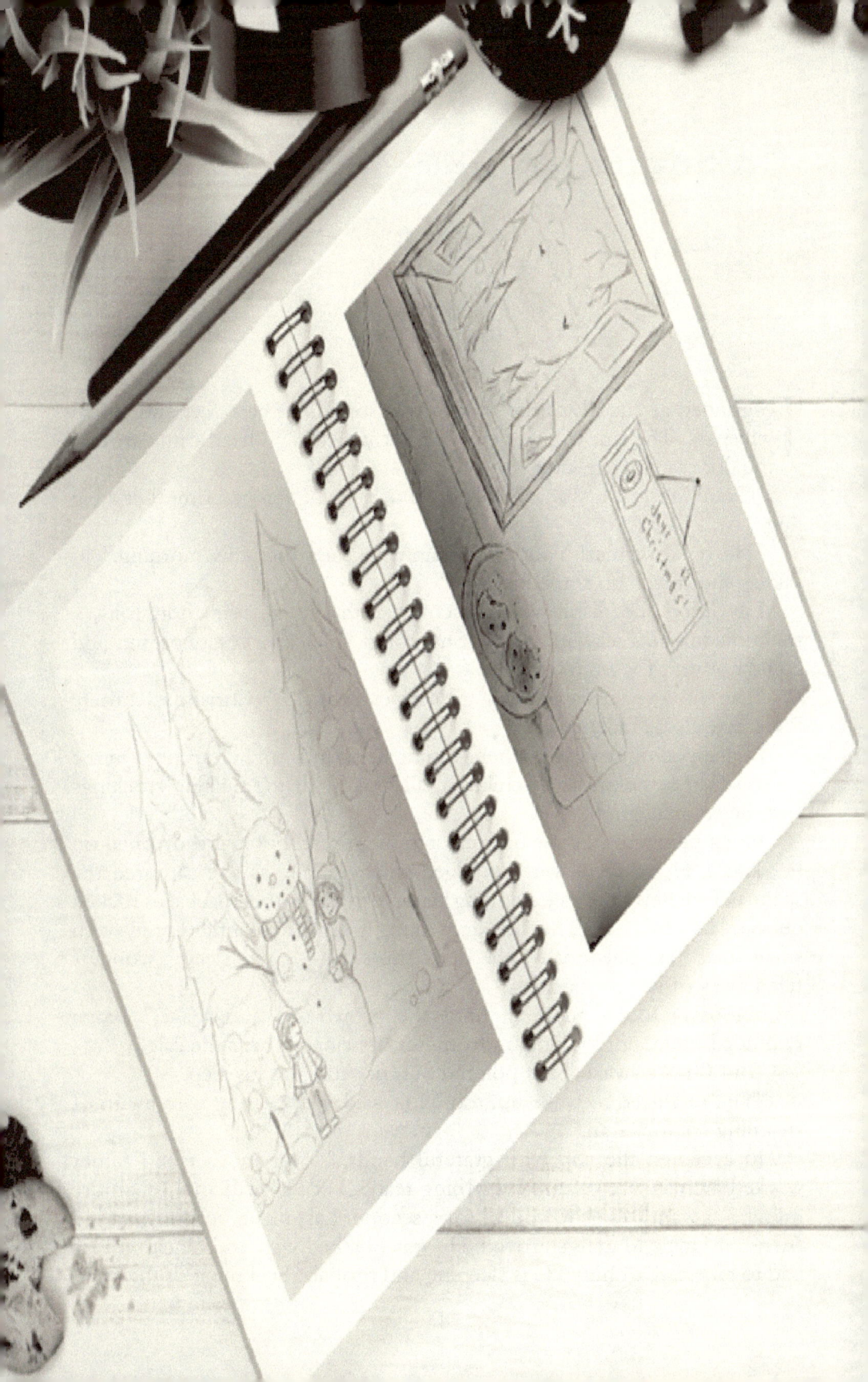

CHAPTER 4: CHRISTMAS MORNING

J o grinned as she heard the first furtive sounds of bare feet and stifled whispers. The sun was not even up yet when Lily's head came around the doorway of the kitchen.

"Gran! Merry Christmas!" Lily cried out, giving her grandmother a big hug.

"Merry Christmas! You are certainly an early bird this morning." Jo said as she stirred up some biscuits.

Lily lifted the dishtowel that covered the rising cinnamon rolls, a tradition in the Callahan family. She could smell the yeasty aroma and could not wait for a bite.

"I am not even close to being the only early bird. It's Christmas....there is a whole flock!" Lily laughed.

Jo stepped out of the kitchen, wiping her hands on her apron. On the staircase sat a multitude of children, all looking at the bulging stockings and the colorful gifts.

Fiona perched near the bottom step, her sketchbook already open on her knees. Her fingers were smudged with graphite as she captured the scene before her...the tree standing sentinel in the corner, packages tucked beneath its branches. The stockings hung from the mantle, lumpy with small treasures. But mostly, she drew the faces—eager, sleepy, wonder-filled faces of her cousins.

"Nobody touch anything until the grown-ups are awake," Fiona reminded them, not looking up from her drawing. "That's the rule."

"But Gran's awake," Ian pointed out, fidgeting on his step.

"The rest need to wake up, too," Lily said, reappearing with a cup of steaming tea for Gran.

Jo accepted the cup with grateful hands. "Your mother and father worked awfully late getting everything ready. Let's give them a few more minutes. I want to talk to you all for a second. Last night, very late, an old friend of Uncle Marcus's arrived. He was in a bad way, and Uncle Tobias had to take care of him. He is sleeping and probably will most of the day."

The children's heads nodded and Max asked. "Is the friend an Army guy?"

"A Marine, and yes, he is," Jo replied. "I will send all of you off to wake your parents when I am done with my tea."

Fiona's pencil caught the way the pre-dawn light filtered through the windows, painting silver-blue shadows across the floor. She sketched quickly, knowing these quiet moments wouldn't last once the chaos of Christmas morning truly began.

"What's that smell?" Jake whispered from his perch halfway up the stairs.

"Cinnamon rolls," Merryn answered, her eyes bright. "Gran always makes them for Christmas."

"And biscuits," added Lily, "for the grown-ups who don't have a sweet tooth."

Fiona smiled to herself as she drew. This was Christmas now, whispering on staircases, waiting for cinnamon rolls, the anticipation almost better than the presents themselves. She wanted to remember it all, exactly as it was.

Jo sipped her tea slowly. Too slow as far as the grandchildren were concerned. Setting her cup on the counter with a few sips left in it, Jo went to check the cinnamon rolls and get the coffee started. Glancing into the dining area she saw Edwin peek into her cup and then shake his head sadly at Jake and Max.

Chuckling, she strolled out into the room and picked up her cup. All eyes shifted to the cup...willing it to her lips. Ever so slowly, she began to move it toward her mouth. The anticipation was palpable. Suddenly, she tipped the cup back and drained the rest of the tea in one gulp.

"Go get them!" she laughed, and the children headed to wake their parents and the other adults.

A thundering of feet echoed through the lodge as children scattered in all directions. Lily and Ian darted upstairs, while Fiona and Rowan raced to their parents' room on the main floor. Max, Jake and Sadie led the pack to Father Tom's room. Squeals and protests mingled with sleepy groans as the adults were dragged from warm beds.

Fiona burst into her parents' room without knocking. "It's Christmas! Gran finished her tea! Come on!"

Beth pulled the quilt over her head. "Five more minutes."

"That never works," Boone mumbled, already sitting up and reaching for his slippers.

Downstairs, Jo pulled the cinnamon rolls from the oven, their sweet aroma filling the kitchen. The scent worked magic that even the children couldn't match; adults appeared in doorways, hair tousled and eyes bleary, but smiles creeping across their faces.

Gus shuffled into the kitchen and wrapped his arms around Jo from behind. "Merry Christmas, love."

"Fifty years of Christmas mornings together," Jo whispered, leaning back against him. "And they still can't wait for me to finish my tea."

In the living room, the children formed a restless circle around the tree, whispering and pointing at packages. Lily stationed herself by the stockings, straightening them with excited anticipation. Fiona abandoned her sketchbook to help, though her fingers itched to capture the scene – the way sunlight now streamed through frosted windows, how Aunt Mary's hair fell loose and dark around her shoulders, Uncle Owen's mismatched socks.

"Everyone here?" Franklin called, counting heads as bleary-eyed adults filed into the living room.

"Almost," Clare answered, pouring coffee into waiting mugs. "Father Tom is coming. Tobias is checking on their guest and getting Marcus and Deb, then he'll be along."

Cinnamon rolls and biscuits were passed out with coffee, tea and milk to help make the waiting a little more bearable.

The waiting was exquisite torture for the children, but Fiona caught Gran's eye and saw something there; a quiet joy in this moment of suspended anticipation, when possibility hung in the air like magic.

* * *

Finally, Tobias slipped into the room, followed by Marcus and Deb. They settled into the last remaining spaces as Gus stood by the tree, ready to begin the gift distribution.

"Christmas isn't about what's under the tree," he said, his voice warm and rough in the morning light. "It's about who's gathered around it. And look at us…all together."

Franklin and Boone began passing out gifts, calling names, and delivering packages wrapped in fabric scraps, old maps, and pages from catalogs. The rustle of improvised wrapping paper filled the air as eager hands tore into presents.

Fiona squeezed Lily's hand tight, their special gift still hidden behind them. They watched, hearts beating fast, as the others opened their presents.

"Look what Quinn made!" Merryn shrieked, holding up a set of wooden blocks painted with animals and letters. She immediately dumped them onto the floor, arranging them into towers that tottered and fell.

Lucy's eyes grew round as saucers when she unwrapped a small ragdoll with yarn hair and button eyes. "For me?" she whispered, clutching it to her chest.

"Gemma and I made her," Leah explained. "Her dress comes off so you can change her clothes."

Lucy hugged the doll tighter. "I'm gonna name her Star."

Jake whistled when he opened a corner shelf whittled from pine. "This is awesome! I can put all of my river rock collection on this," he exclaimed, running his fingers over the smooth edges. "Thanks, Uncle Owen!"

Sadie received a knitted hat that matched her eyes, while Rowan unwrapped a new journal bound in leather scraps. There were whittled figurines, clay pots with wobbly rims, socks knitted from unraveled sweaters, and shirts sewn from old linens.

Ian squealed over a wooden train with cars that actually rolled, and Ruth gasped at a bracelet made from polished stones. Max received a slingshot that Uncle Boone promised to teach him to use "far away from windows," making everyone laugh.

Everywhere Fiona looked, she saw joy; not because the gifts were fancy or expensive, but because each one carried love in every stitch, every cut, every brushstroke. She watched Gran's face, soft with happiness as she observed her family, and knew that their gift would be perfect.

"Gran and Pop will love ours....I can't wait," Lily whispered, nudging Fiona. "It's almost time."

Fiona nodded, heart fluttering like a bird. Their gift might not be as practical as a shelf or as fun as blocks, but they'd poured their hearts into it. And somehow, that felt exactly right.

* * *

When the wrapping paper was smoothed and the little quilt gift wraps were folded neatly in a box for the next time gifts were given, the women headed to the kitchen to get breakfast started. Fiona and Lily still sat, waiting for the perfect time.

"Maybe when everyone sits down to breakfast?" Fiona asked.

"Oh! That is a good idea, everyone will be in one place and can see." Lily agreed.

The bundle remained hidden behind them, wrapped in one of the pretty quilts and secured with a piece of twine Fiona had salvaged from Uncle Owen's workshop. They watched as Aunt Beth carried baby Luke toward the kitchen, followed by Mary balancing a stack of plates.

Pop lingered by the tree, adjusting a wooden ornament that had slipped sideways on its branch. "You two plotting something?" he asked without turning around, his weathered hands gentle on the decorations.

Fiona's eyes widened. "How did you know?"

Pop laughed, the sound warming the room like another log on the fire. "Sixty-plus years on this earth teaches a man to recognize the sound of whispering children with secrets." He turned, eyebrows raised in question.

Lily looked at Fiona, who nodded. "We made something for you and Gran," Lily said. "But we want everyone to see it."

"Well then," Pop said, tapping his finger against his nose. "Your secret's safe with me."

The smell of bacon and coffee filled the lodge as they waited, watching the younger children play with their new treasures. Ian ran his wooden train along the floor, making locomotive sounds. Ruth showed her stone bracelet to everyone who passed. The normalcy of it all, children playing on Christmas morning, made the world feel right again, even without electricity or stores or anything that had once seemed so necessary.

"Breakfast!" Gran called from the kitchen doorway. "Everyone, wash up and find a seat."

Chairs scraped and benches creaked as the family gathered around the long table. Platters of golden cinnamon rolls dripping with honey sat alongside bowls of preserved fruit and pitchers of milk. Steam rose from mugs of coffee and pine tea, curling toward the ceiling.

"Now?" Fiona whispered, clutching their package.

Lily nodded, her stomach fluttering with butterflies. "Now."

They rose together, the bundle held between them, and walked to the head of the table where Gran and Pop sat. The conversations died away as curious faces turned toward them.

"We made something," Lily began, her voice stronger than she expected. "A gift for Gran and Pop."

"But really for everyone," Fiona added quickly.

They placed the package in front of Gran, whose eyes crinkled with surprise. "For us? You sneaky little foxes."

"Open it," Lily urged, bouncing slightly on her toes. "Please."

Gran's fingers worked at the twine as Pop leaned in close. The fabric fell away, revealing a book bound with strips of cardboard and leather, its pages uneven but carefully stitched together.

"The First Christmas After," Gran read the title aloud, her voice catching slightly. "By Lily and Fiona Callahan."

"It's Lily's stories and my drawings," Fiona explained, words tumbling out. "Of everything since the lights went out. All the good parts."

"So we never forget," Lily finished.

"We know there are no cameras or videos anymore, so we decided to be the memory keepers. We are going to do these for each season. This one is just Christmas, though, since it is the first." Fiona said.

* * *

Gran opened the cover, revealing Lily's careful handwriting alongside Fiona's detailed sketch of the family arriving at the lodge with the Christmas tree. The room fell silent as Gran turned the page, her eyes filling with tears.

"Oh my," she whispered, tracing a finger over the drawing of the wagon bringing their pine tree home. Every face was there—Buck's wild beard, Owen's crooked smile, even baby Luke bundled against Judith's chest.

Pop leaned closer, his arm around Gran's shoulders. "Look at that. You've captured us all just right."

Gran read aloud in a voice that trembled slightly: "'December 15th—Today we brought home the biggest tree I've ever seen. Uncle Boone said it was too big, but Pop just laughed and said Christmas trees can never be too big, only doorways can be too small.'"

Laughter rippled around the table. Uncle Boone shook his head, grinning. "Those were my exact words."

"Turn the page, Gran," Fiona urged, her cheeks flushed with excitement.

Gran did, revealing the kitchen scene with flour-covered counters and children helping with Christmas baking. Fiona had drawn Gran standing tall, directing the chaos with a wooden spoon raised like a conductor's baton.

"'Operation Sugar and Spice,'" Gran read, her smile growing wider. "Lily, you've written my words exactly as I said them."

"I wanted to get it right," Lily said. "For the future."

Page after page revealed their family story: the ornament box opening, Pop's tall tales by the fire, Buck showing Fiona how to whittle, and Mary teaching the younger children to wrap gifts in fabric. Each memory captured in words and pictures, preserving what might otherwise have faded with time.

When Gran reached the scene of Pop reading 'Twas the Night Before Christmas, a tear slipped down her cheek and dropped onto the page. Pop reached out quickly, dabbing it away with his handkerchief.

"Don't want to smudge Fiona's beautiful work," he said gruffly, though his own eyes glistened.

The family crowded closer, peering over shoulders and standing on tiptoes to see the pages. Uncle Franklin lifted Ian so he could see better.

"That's me!" Ian pointed excitedly at a drawing of himself stringing pine cones.

"And look here," Mary said, her voice warm. "Fiona drew the way the candles made shadows dance on the ceiling. I'd forgotten that already. At this rate, you will far surpass my artistic talent!"

Gran turned to the final page, where Lily had written:

This is just the beginning of our story. The lights may have gone out in the world, but they're still burning bright here at the Lodge. We're going to keep writing it all down—spring, summer, fall, and winter—so years from now, we'll remember not what we lost, but what we found.

Below it, Fiona had drawn their entire family gathered around the Christmas tree, faces illuminated by candle glow, smiles bright despite the darkness beyond their windows.

"This," Gran said, pressing her palm flat against the page, "is the most precious gift I've ever received."

Pop nodded, unable to speak for a moment.

"It's our new family history book," Gran continued, looking around the table at each face. "When we're old and gray…"

"Mmmm…Older and grayer," Pop corrected with a wink.

"When we're older and grayer," Gran amended with a smile, "we'll open these pages and remember exactly how it felt to discover what really matters."

Lily and Fiona exchanged glances, their faces glowing with pride and happiness.

"The girls have given us something electricity could never power," Pop said, his voice strong again. "They've given us our story back."

The Callahan's will be back!

kellyschweigerbook.com

If you enjoy this series, please consider leaving a review. Please consider donating this book to your local library or share with a friend when you are done.

ABOUT THE AUTHOR

 **KELLY SCHWEIGER** lives tucked among the hills, fields, and trees of upstate NY, where stories grow wild and the seasons write their own poetry. A lifelong lover of quiet places and fierce characters, she writes fiction that explores resilience, family, and the unbreakable thread between land and heart. When not writing, Kelly can be found relaxing with her loving husband, Fred, playing with her grandchildren, foraging for 'lawn salad', reading, or drinking too much coffee with her cats curled at her feet. This is her debut novel, although she has published several cookbooks and children's books in the past.

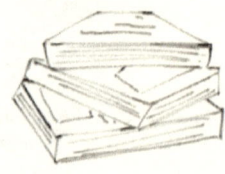

ACKNOWLEDGEMENTS

I am forever grateful for all of the love and encouragement of the people who kept believing in this book, this Universe, and in me, on the hard days.

To my family, both by blood and by bond: thank you for your strength, your stories, and your endless supply of patience. Thank you for sharing your knowledge and the small bits of your personality that made it into my characters.

I want to especially thank my husband for standing by me through all of my adventures, projects, and my endless chaos. I love you forever, and ever, amen.

Most of all, thank you, dear reader, for walking this path with me. I'm so glad you're here.

Love this book? Tip &
message the author
with **Quilltips!**